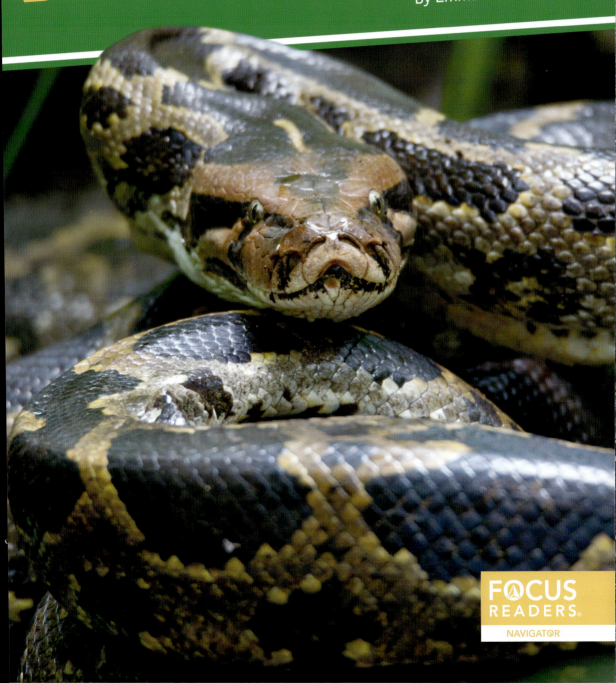

INVASIVE SPECIES
BURMESE PYTHONS

by Emma Huddleston

FOCUS READERS®
NAVIGATOR

WWW.FOCUSREADERS.COM

Copyright © 2022 by Focus Readers®, Lake Elmo, MN 55042. All rights reserved. No part of this book may be reproduced or utilized in any form or by any means without written permission from the publisher.

Focus Readers is distributed by North Star Editions:
sales@northstareditions.com | 888-417-0195

Produced for Focus Readers by Red Line Editorial.

Content Consultant: Peter C. Iacono, United States Geological Survey

Photographs ©: Shutterstock Images, cover, 1, 8–9, 11, 16–17, 19 (American coot), 19 (squirrel, rabbit, rat, mouse), 19 (wren); Bryan Falk/USGS, 4–5; USGS, 7; Red Line Editorial, 13; Everglades National Park, 15; iStockphoto, 19 (raccoon, opossum, alligator, ibis), 19 (little blue heron); Robert Krayer/NPS Photo, 21; Manuel Balce Ceneta/AP Images, 22–23; Florida Fish and Wildlife Conservation Commission, 25; Mike Gauldin/USGS, 27; Gaia Meigs-Friend/USGS, 29

Library of Congress Cataloging-in-Publication Data
Names: Huddleston, Emma, author.
Title: Burmese pythons / by Emma Huddleston.
Description: Lake Elmo, MN : Focus Readers, [2022] | Series: Invasive species | Includes index. | Audience: Grades 4-6
Identifiers: LCCN 2021003727 (print) | LCCN 2021003728 (ebook) | ISBN 9781644938546 (hardcover) | ISBN 9781644939000 (paperback) | ISBN 9781644939468 (ebook) | ISBN 9781644939871 (pdf)
Subjects: LCSH: Burmese python--Juvenile literature. | Introduced reptiles--Juvenile literature. | Pest introduction--Juvenile literature. | Nature--Effect of human beings on--Juvenile literature.
Classification: LCC QL666.O63 H83 2022 (print) | LCC QL666.O63 (ebook) | DDC 597.96/78--dc23
LC record available at https://lccn.loc.gov/2021003727
LC ebook record available at https://lccn.loc.gov/2021003728

Printed in the United States of America
Mankato, MN
082021

ABOUT THE AUTHOR
Emma Huddleston enjoys being a children's book author. When she's not writing, she can be found reading or running outside. She lives in Minnesota with her husband.

TABLE OF CONTENTS

CHAPTER 1
Massive Snake 5

CHAPTER 2
From Pet to Problem 9

THAT'S AMAZING!
Squeezing to Death 14

CHAPTER 3
Fierce Predator 17

CHAPTER 4
Stopping Their Spread 23

Focus on Burmese Pythons • 30
Glossary • 31
To Learn More • 32
Index • 32

CHAPTER 1

MASSIVE SNAKE

Grasses shiver in Everglades National Park in Florida. A Burmese python slithers past. The snake's body seems to go on and on. It is more than 18 feet (5.5 m) long. The Burmese python is one of the five largest snakes on Earth.

A marsh rabbit hops through the grasses nearby. It is looking for food.

The Burmese python is tan with dark spots. A dark, pointed shape marks its head.

It moves closer to the hidden snake. The rabbit's scent grows stronger and stronger. Quickly, the snake jolts forward. Its sharp teeth grab the rabbit. Next, the python's body twists around its prey. Then, the snake squeezes. Soon, the snake swallows the rabbit whole.

PEOPLE AND PYTHONS

People in Florida have found Burmese pythons near their homes. In 2019, a 16-foot (4.9-m) python was removed from under someone's house. The snake's nest held nearly 50 unhatched eggs. The eggs were removed, too. However, Burmese pythons usually don't seek out humans' homes. They prefer wild places. They will avoid people if they can.

Burmese pythons are hard to spot in the wild. Their patterned skin often blends in with their surroundings.

Marsh rabbits are one of many **species** that Burmese pythons hunt in the Everglades. As a result, marsh rabbits are disappearing. Other small animals are, too. Pythons are taking over.

CHAPTER 2

FROM PET TO PROBLEM

Burmese pythons are native to jungles and grassy marshlands in Southeast Asia. They can also be found in nearby regions. These snakes are fierce hunters. They are most active at night. The heaviest ones weigh up to 200 pounds (91 kg). Females are larger than males.

Burmese pythons often climb trees in order to bask in the sun.

Burmese pythons mainly eat birds and small **mammals**. They also hunt frogs, toads, and bats. But they have poor eyesight. So, the snakes hunt by sensing heat. They can also smell nearby prey. Native prey have developed ways of living with Burmese pythons. As a result,

LIVING ALONE

Burmese pythons live alone. They start coming together to mate in late fall. Mating continues through the winter. In the spring, female pythons lay up to 100 eggs. For two to three months, they sit on and around the eggs. Mothers don't eat while caring for the eggs. They lose up to 40 percent of their body weight.

Burmese pythons are great swimmers. They can stay underwater for 30 minutes before needing a breath of air.

the prey populations remain stable. This process is common among native predators and prey. It is one kind of **co-evolution**.

However, python numbers are dropping in their native **habitats**. Humans are the main reason for this drop. Habitat loss and illegal hunting are two major threats.

People hunt Burmese pythons for their skin. Sometimes people use parts of the snakes in medicine. Some people eat their meat, too.

People have also taken the pythons to new areas. In the 1970s, the snakes became part of the pet trade. People brought more than 100,000 Burmese pythons to the United States as pets. Some of the snakes escaped. Others were not cared for properly. Some owners released them into the wild.

In 1979, people first spotted a Burmese python in the Florida Everglades. By the 1990s, the snakes were having babies there on their own. By 2020, they had spread through more than 1,000 square miles (2,600 sq km) of Florida. Pythons had also reached islands in the Florida Keys. People have even found them in Puerto Rico.

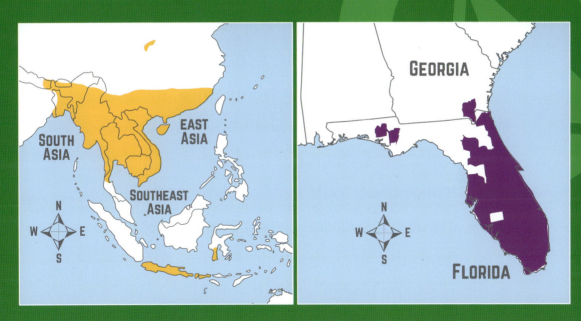

BURMESE PYTHON RANGE

NATIVE RANGE — INVASIVE RANGE

THAT'S AMAZING!

SQUEEZING TO DEATH

Burmese pythons can eat up to 25 percent of their body weight in one meal. Some can even eat whole deer or 7-foot (2.1-m) alligators.

A Burmese python kills by squeezing its prey. First, the snake bites an animal. It uses six rows of sharp teeth. Next, the snake wraps itself around its prey. Each time the animal breathes, the snake tightens its wrap. Then, it swallows prey whole.

The Burmese python has **flexible** jaws. It can open its mouth up to three times wider than its body. Inside the python, strong stomach **acids** break down the food over time. For this reason, pythons can go weeks without eating.

A Burmese python battles an alligator in the Florida Everglades.

CHAPTER 3

FIERCE PREDATOR

Burmese pythons are one of the worst invasive species in the United States. They harm Florida **food webs** for many reasons. First, these snakes face few natural predators there. No animals limit the pythons' numbers. Also, female pythons lay up to 100 eggs at a time. As a result, python numbers grow quickly.

After hatching, Burmese pythons often live for 20 to 25 years.

This growth causes problems for native animals. For example, Burmese pythons hunt high numbers of native animals. In the Everglades, they have cut down mammal populations. Between 2003 and 2011, scientists kept track of mammals there. They compared these sightings with counts from the 1990s.

In the 2000s, people found far fewer raccoons, opossums, and bobcats. People came across those animals up to 99 percent less often than before. In some cases, people came across no foxes or rabbits at all. These decreases all happened when python numbers were growing. For this reason, scientists believed the snakes had caused those animal numbers to drop.

Pythons can change all parts of a food web. In the Everglades, for instance,

THE DIET OF A BURMESE PYTHON

For a Burmese python to grow to 13 feet (4.0 m) in the Everglades, it would need to eat this many animals over the course of five to seven years.

1 opossum
1 raccoon
4 alligators
5 American coots
6 little blue herons
8 ibises
10 squirrels
15 rabbits
15 wrens
30 cotton rats
72 mice

raccoons eat turtle eggs. As Burmese pythons reduce raccoon numbers, turtle populations could rise. But more turtles could cause other changes.

In addition, Burmese pythons can create more than one problem for native animals. For example, pythons

SPREADING DISEASE

Burmese pythons can spread disease to new areas. For instance, one kind of worm often attaches to a python. The worm drinks the snake's blood to stay alive. But this doesn't kill the snake. The snake carries the worm from place to place. In a new area, the worm attaches to a native snake. Native snakes have no defense against it. The worm can get in the snake's lungs and kill it.

In the Florida Everglades, Burmese pythons may threaten many kinds of native wading birds, such as green herons.

hunt white-tailed deer and alligators. The snakes also eat the same food as alligators and raccoons. So, the snakes threaten those animals in two ways.

Many plants and animals live in the Everglades. Food webs are difficult to understand. It is hard to know every change Burmese pythons will cause.

CHAPTER 4

STOPPING THEIR SPREAD

By the 2010s, Burmese pythons were thriving in southern Florida. Governments took action. In 2012, the United States banned bringing Burmese pythons into the country. In 2020, Florida stopped allowing people to keep the snakes as pets. These laws aimed to slow the spread of pythons.

In 2009, a lawmaker brought a dead Burmese python to the US Congress to show the problem of pythons in Florida.

However, laws cannot get rid of snakes already in the wild. So, Florida officials encouraged people to catch and hunt Burmese pythons. In some places, they held python-hunting events. People competed to catch pythons. Some won prizes, too. In 2017, Florida began training teams to catch invasive snakes. The state paid these teams for their work. By 2020, hunters had caught at least 5,000 pythons.

People use different methods to find the snakes. For example, dogs can help find the snakes. Dogs can learn the smell of a Burmese python. Then they can detect that smell in the wild.

On June 25, 2019, members of a Florida python team caught the team's 500th Burmese python.

Radio tracking is another common method. First, scientists catch a male python. Next, they place a small device inside the snake's body. This tracker sends out radio signals. Then, scientists release the snake. They use a receiver to pick up the tracker's signals. Those signals show where the snake is moving.

In 2019, scientists tagged 40 Burmese pythons with trackers. They learned where those snakes lived and bred. The tagged snakes were helpful. Scientists

THE PYTHON BOWL

In January 2020, hundreds of people took part in the Python Bowl. It was a 10-day snake-catching event in Florida. Several groups helped organize it. Organizers wanted to let people help solve the problem of Burmese pythons. People caught 80 Burmese pythons. The event also spread awareness about the snakes.

Scientists insert a radio tracking device into a Burmese python.

had captured more than 80 adult pythons by 2020. They had also caught 2,500 developing eggs by May 2020.

However, Burmese pythons are hard to study. They are **elusive**. In addition, the pythons live in a very large area of land in Florida. Searching the land takes lots of time and resources.

Scientists are working on finding new ways to track the snakes. One method has worked well for pythons. Animals often leave traces of their bodies as they travel. Their skin may shed. Or they may leave spit. Skin and spit contain an animal's **DNA**. Scientists can tell if it's a Burmese python based on the DNA.

Pythons often leave their DNA in the water. So, scientists take **samples** of water in Florida. They study that water. Sometimes they find python DNA in the samples. Then they know that the snake traveled through that area. This method lets scientists track the snakes without having to catch any.

A scientist works in the lab to test a water sample for Burmese python DNA.

Stopping the spread of Burmese pythons is the best option. It is easier than trying to get rid of a population after it settles in a new area. New tracking methods and more data will help scientists control python populations. The government and experts are working hard to slow the python's spread.

FOCUS ON
BURMESE PYTHONS

Write your answers on a separate piece of paper.

1. Write a sentence that describes the main ideas of Chapter 2.

2. Do you think people will be able to get rid of Burmese pythons in Florida? Why or why not?

3. When did the United States ban people from bringing Burmese pythons into the country?
    - **A.** 2003
    - **B.** 2012
    - **C.** 2020

4. What is one reason that makes Burmese pythons hard to find?
    - **A.** They blend in with their environment.
    - **B.** They can grow incredibly long.
    - **C.** They often approach humans.

Answer key on page 32.

GLOSSARY

acids
Strong chemicals that can break things down.

co-evolution
The process of two or more species changing over a long period of time in response to one another.

DNA
The genetic material in the cells of living organisms.

elusive
Able to avoid being found, tracked, or caught.

flexible
Easy to bend or change.

food webs
The feeding relationships among different living things.

habitats
The types of places where plants or animals grow or live.

mammals
Animals that have hair and produce milk for their young.

samples
Small pieces taken from a larger object for study.

species
Groups of animals or plants that are alike and can breed with one another.

TO LEARN MORE

BOOKS

Hamilton, S. L. *Pythons*. Minneapolis: Abdo Publishing, 2019.

Messner, Kate. *Tracking Pythons: The Quest to Catch an Invasive Predator and Save an Ecosystem*. Minneapolis: Lerner Publishing Group, 2020.

Spalding, Maddie. *Everglades National Park*. Minneapolis: Abdo Publishing, 2017.

NOTE TO EDUCATORS

Visit **www.focusreaders.com** to find lesson plans, activities, links, and other resources related to this title.

INDEX

alligators, 14, 19, 21

birds, 10

deer, 14, 21
disease, 20
DNA, 28

East Asia, 13
eggs, 6, 10, 17, 20, 27
Everglades National Park, 5, 7, 12, 18–19, 21

Florida, 5–6, 12–13, 17, 23–24, 26–28
Florida Keys, 13

Georgia, 13

mammals, 10, 18

Puerto Rico, 13
Python Bowl, 26

rabbits, 5–7, 18–19
raccoons, 18–21

South Asia, 13
Southeast Asia, 9, 13

trackers, 25–26
turtles, 20

United States, 12, 17, 23

Answer Key: 1. Answers will vary; 2. Answers will vary; 3. B; 4. A